The Adventures of RATMAN

By Ellen Weiss and Mel Friedman

Illustrated by Dirk Zimmer

A STEPPING STONE BOOK

Random House  New York

Library of Congress Cataloging-in-Publication Data
Weiss, Ellen. The adventures of Ratman / by Ellen Weiss and Mel Friedman; illustrations by Dirk Zimmer.   p.   cm. — (A Stepping stone book) Summary: With the help of a rat costume, Tod Watson is transformed from an ordinary eight-year-old into a superhero named Ratman. ISBN 0-679-80531-1 (pbk.) — ISBN 0-679-90531-6 (lib. bdg.) [1. Heroes—Fiction.] I. Friedman, Mel. II. Zimmer, Dirk, ill. III. Title. PZ7.W4472Ad 1990 [Fic]—dc20 89-10869

Manufactured in the United States of America   1 2 3 4 5 6 7 8 9 10

For Eli

CHAPTER 1

You may not believe this, but I am the late, great Ratman. For thirty-seven incredible days I was a superhero. Sort of.

My name is Tod Watson. I live in a town called South Fork. It's almost smack in the center of the United States. There are two banks in South Fork. There are also three gas stations, four churches, and one museum. The museum is called the International Feather Museum. It has all kinds of interesting feathers from around the world. It gets about ten visitors a year.

There's some talk now in South Fork of making a Ratman museum. There wouldn't be very much to put in it, though. A strange-looking metal belt. A bunch of ashes. And maybe a candle from Matty Ritter's ninth birthday cake. He wouldn't even have had a ninth birthday if I hadn't saved his bacon.

It all started on the twenty-eighth of June. The day was shaping up to be a bad one for me. For one thing, it was really hot. We'd been having a drought, and even though it was hardly even summer yet, the grass was burned brown. There wasn't any breeze at all.

For another thing, it was report card day. Now, if I'd been an only child, report card day wouldn't have been so bad. I would have gone home. I would have shown my mom a report card full of Bs, with a sprinkling of B pluses and one B minus. And she would have been just as happy as anything. "My boy Tod," she would have said. "What a smart boy."

Instead my teacher, Mrs. Cooper, handed me my report card with a sweet little smile. "You've improved a lot this year," she said.

Then she waited a moment. "Maybe Pam could help you with your long division over the summer."

Pam. Pam, Pam, Pam, Pam. If I heard my sister's name one more time from a teacher, a neighbor, or even a stranger, I was going to take the next bus to Alaska. I'd go live in an igloo.

It was bad enough having a sister six years older than I was. She was fourteen. That already meant that a *girl* could do every single thing in the world better than me. But on top of that, Pamela Watson was not your average sister. She was perfect.

In fact, Pam the Perfect had never come home with anything less than an A on her report card. She was brilliant, pretty, and nice. She could even play a mean game of tennis.

At the beginning of every school year, every teacher I had would look at me, beaming. "Oh!" they would coo. "How wonderful to have Pamela Watson's brother in my class!" And by the end of the year they would all say, "Maybe Pam can help you with your math."

Or English. Or geography. Or recess. Or lunch.

So, on that June 28, I trudged home with a heavy heart and a heavy report card. I tripped on the cracked sidewalk in front of the candy store. That was no big surprise. I always tripped once or twice on the way home. I am not very athletic.

I walked into the kitchen and found Pam there, talking on the phone. She was about to leave for tennis camp. That meant she had to get in all her phone time with her girlfriends quick. She put in at least fourteen hours a day.

She waved at me and I waved back. Then I opened the refrigerator.

I was hot, I was thirsty, and I was in luck. There was a great big bottle of grape juice right on the shelf.

I took out the bottle, heaved it up onto the kitchen counter, and started trying to twist open the cap. It was hard.

Without missing a beat in her conversation, Pam walked over to me. She hitched up her shoulder to cradle the phone, took the grape juice bottle out of my hands, and opened it. Then she handed it back to me and walked away.

So there I was. Standing there. You see, it wasn't that Pam meant to make me feel like a two-year-old. It was just that she was so used to doing things for me, ever since I was a baby, that it had never occurred to her to stop.

I hadn't even presented my report card to my mom, and already it was a terrible day.

I decided to go up to my room and loll around. There wasn't any more homework for the year, so I was free. I could lie on my bed, daydream, stare out the window, or read comics—all the things I liked to do best.

Up in my room I flipped through the stack of comic books next to my bed. I was very familiar with them. I spent quite a bit of time on my bed, reading my comics. My mother thought they were rotting my brain. "The only good thing about comic books," she'd sigh, "is that they're quieter than TV."

She was probably right. They are quieter. But then, so is twiddling your thumbs.

Wait a second. What was this? I pulled a comic book out of the pile.

Amazing Tales.

Where had it come from? I didn't remember buying it. Maybe I had gotten it in that last batch I traded with my best friend, Matty. Matty is a good kid, but he has some pretty awful comic books.

Amazing Tales looked really boring. The superheroes were badly drawn, and the way they talked was strange and old-fashioned.

"Gee whillikers," one of them said in a speech balloon. "That Mr. Destructo is a tough customer." Give me a break, I thought.

There were all kinds of ads in the back, for things like x-ray glasses, 3-D glow-in-the-dark stickers, and real dinosaur teeth. Things no kid should be without.

Then a tiny ad at the bottom of the page caught my eye.

"Send away now," it said, "for the adventure of your life. You can be a hero. This is no joke."

Strange. I had never seen this ad before in any of my comics.

Be a hero.

"Well, what the heck," I said out loud. "I don't have much else to do this summer. I might as well be a hero." I wrote my name and address in the tiny blanks in the ad. Whatever they sent back would probably be funny. I could laugh about it with Matty.

I cut the little square out of the comic book and put it into an envelope. I put a stamp on it, walked down to the mailbox, and dropped it in.

CHAPTER 2

About half an hour later, I was lying on my bed again. I was trying to remember the name of every single pitcher in the American League. This is why my mother often said to me, "Tod, if you used half the brainpower in school that you use on baseball and comic books, you'd be in college already."

My concentration was shattered by the doorbell.

"PAM!" I shouted. "CAN YOU GET THE DOOR?" I was much too busy to run downstairs and see who it was.

BING-BONG! It seemed even louder than usual. Pam must have gone out. Rats.

I ran down the stairs two at a time. (Pam, of course, could do three at a time. I had tried three at a time once. I'd sprained my ankle.)

When I opened the door, the guy who delivers our packages was there. Or rather, he was *like* the guy who delivers our packages. He had on a blue uniform, not a brown one. And I had never seen him before.

"Package for Tod Watson," he said. "Sign here."

"A package for me?" I was surprised. "Who's it from?"

"Don't ask me," said the man. "You sent for it." He handed me the paper to sign.

I glanced at his truck. It was blue, like his uniform, not brown. UPS, it said on the side. Then, in smaller letters, UNUSUAL POSTAL SERVICE.

Unusual Postal Service? Hmmm. . . .

I'd only sent away for something once in the past year—half an hour ago. This couldn't be that—could it?

I signed the paper. "Why isn't there a return address on it?" I asked.

"I don't answer questions, kid," he said. "I just deliver." Then he took the paper back, gave me a funny little salute, and left.

I stared at the box on the floor. Should I open it? I was just about to when Pam came up the front walk. She was loaded down with shopping bags.

"Can you help me with these?" she asked

"Sure," I said. I took a few bags from her. "What's in here?"

"Just a few last-minute items for tennis camp," she said. "Hair gel, socks, new bathing suit . . ."

"You really need all this stuff?" I asked.

"I just want everything to be right," she said. If it was anybody else, I'd have thought maybe she was nervous about going. But not perfect, polished, popular Pam. Couldn't be.

For the next two hours Pam packed and I helped. Then my mom came home. Her arms were full of dried flowers and leaves. She makes wreaths out of them and sells them to flower shops. She has plenty of orders.

"We'd better run for the camp bus, Pam," Mom said. "It's leaving in twenty minutes."

"Omigosh!" gasped Pam. She threw her arms around me, kissed me hard, and ran for the door. "I'll miss you!" she called.

"I have to go to the supermarket on the way home, Tod," my mother said as she left. "Do you want to come along?"

"No, thanks." I kind of like being by my-self.

"Okay," she said. "You know Mrs. Stone is next door if you need her." Mrs. Stone is ninety-two years old, but her house is always full of fresh-baked cookies.

"I know, Mom," I said. " 'Bye!"

The door slammed for the last time, and they were gone.

It was suddenly quiet in the house. I looked around, trying to decide what to do with the rest of my summer. And then I remembered the box.

It was still standing next to the front door. I took it up to my room. A strange feeling told me to close my door.

I sat on the bed. Of course it was just my imagination, but the box seemed to be giving off some weird kind of energy, as if it was calling to me. "Tod," it seemed to be calling. "Open me. Open me now."

Well, what could I do? I opened the box.

Inside, neatly folded, was a garment. I took it out of the box. A small pink piece of paper fell to the floor. "CONGRATULATIONS," it said. "YOU ARE ABOUT TO BECOME A HERO."

"You are now Ratman," it went on. "You will be Ratman for thirty-seven days. Use your powers wisely. Do good, not evil. Wash suit in cold water only."

I took a good look at the suit. It looked a little like pajamas, the kind with feet. It was brown and fuzzy, and it had these huge ears and a long, ratty tail. It zipped up the front.

What kind of dumb joke was this anyhow? Somebody was trying to play a trick on me. But who? And why had this thing come half an hour after I'd mailed in the coupon?

Okay, I thought. Maybe—just maybe—something's actually going on here. Let's say I'm going to be Ratman. If I'm going to do it for thirty-seven days (which I'm sure I'm not), that means I'll be Ratman until . . . Let's see . . . thirty days hath September, June, July, and November . . . I'll be Ratman until August 4. Of course I'm not going to *be* Ratman, because this is too ridiculous.

I stared at the suit for a minute. Nobody

was home. If I tried it on, just for a second, no one would ever know.

I tried the suit on and looked at myself in the mirror. I had big ears and a ratty tail and fuzzy, brownish fur. I looked like a total jerk.

CHAPTER 3

Thank goodness no one will ever see me like this, I thought. Then I noticed something strange.

I could hear things.

I don't just mean I could hear the cars honking outside on Pine Street or the fan whirring in my room. I mean I was *hearing* things. Lots of things. At first the noises were a loud, confusing jumble. Then I realized that if I thought about it, I could sort them out. Soon I could hear dozens of separate noises: glass breaking, a car starting, a baby crying, a cough, a woman humming, a door slamming. I was hearing noises from all over town.

Then I heard a voice I knew. "Oh, yeah?" it was saying. "Well, for your information, I can *too* swim that far."

It was my friend Matty! But where was he? And who was he talking to?

"Oh, no, you can't," said another voice. "Because you're a baby, and babies can't swim that far. They need their mommies to help them." It was Pinky! Pinky was the worst bully in our school. He had a pink face and freckles, and he was big and mean. In short, Pinky was a creep. His greatest joy in life was making people miserable.

"Babies have to wear those cute little plastic water wings," said Pinky in a creepy, teasing voice. "Babies can *wade* in Pine Lake. But not *swim* in it. And forget about swimming *across* it."

Was Pinky crazy? It sounded like he was challenging Matty to swim across Pine Lake! There was no way a kid could get all the way across that lake. It was too big. Besides, everybody knew that the middle was full of freezing cold pockets, where the water was really, really deep. Nobody went out there. Pinky couldn't force him into trying it. Could he?

"Yeah, well, I'm not a baby. I'm going to swim across the lake—right now." I could just about hear Matty's lower lip trembling.

The next thing I heard was a splash, and Pinky laughing. It was a mean, rotten laugh.

Then I heard Matty swimming. I listened hard. Could Matty do it? What would happen if he reached the middle of the lake and got tired? Or cold?

I stood there, nailed to the spot.

Stroke, stroke, stroke, stroke. Matty was doing okay so far.

Then he swallowed a little water, gasped for breath, and coughed. He kept swimming, but he was slower now. Pinky laughed again. Matty was breathing pretty hard.

Then I heard something awful. I heard it so clearly, it was almost as if I was seeing it. I heard Matty's head go under. Then he was flailing around in the water, trying to stay afloat. He'd go under, then come up for air, gasping and choking.

This was horrible. I could hear it all, but what could I do? Was my best friend going to drown right before my ears?

Then it hit me. I was Ratman. If I could hear all this stuff, I really *was* Ratman. Maybe I could save Matty. It didn't seem possible. The lake was a half a mile out of town, and Matty was losing strength every second. Besides, I had no idea what kinds of powers I had. But I had to try.

My room is on the second floor. There is a drainpipe right outside my window, going down to the ground.

I climbed out my window. The height was scary. But I had to get to Matty. I grabbed on to the drainpipe and slid. Then, about half-way down, something very strange happened. I felt different. I felt . . . weightless. It was the strangest feeling I'd ever had. I let go of the drainpipe. And I flew.

It was amazing. I had had dreams about flying. In them I had been soaring high above the world, looking down. This was different. I was moving very fast, skimming over the ground, about six feet up.

I had to watch out for buildings, trees, telephone poles, and tall people. The ground whizzing under me made me dizzy. I tried flapping my arms. That made me go even faster. I was out of the neighborhood now, really zooming along.

Well, it seemed like I covered that half-mile to the lake in about half a minute. It was incredible.

I got to the far end of the lake just as Matty went under again. I could hear that he was struggling. I knew he couldn't see me, and neither could Pinky. Pinky was too far away.

Just as I was about to go into the water, I wondered: Can I swim with this suit on? I had no idea. I seemed to be able to fly at an amazing speed. But that didn't mean I could swim. Maybe the rat suit would weigh me down when it got wet. I could drown five feet from shore!

But there was no time to worry. I slipped under the water.

I *could* swim! Not only that, I could swim incredibly fast! I glided past a lot of surprised fish and was at the center of the lake in no time at all. I didn't even have to go up for air.

And I had a plan, too. I could save Matty, and I could do it so no one saw me. Then it would look as if Matty had swum the lake all by himself. I just had to stay underwater, out of sight. So as soon as I reached Matty, I came up under him and grabbed the waistband of his trunks. Then I struck out for shore, swimming like an arrow. I could hear Matty gulping for air and coughing. Luckily he was too tired to struggle. He just let me pull him along.

In a moment we had reached the shore. I kind of pushed Matty onto the sand. He lay there, gasping.

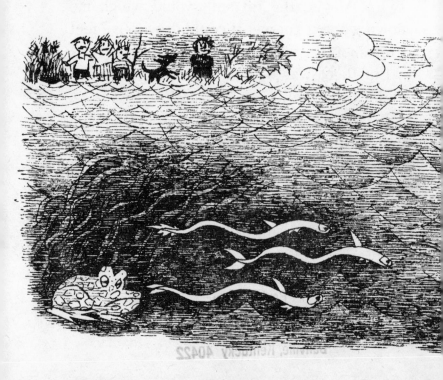

I stayed below the surface of the water, trying to figure out how I could get away. I didn't want anyone to see me in the Ratman suit. Wearing it made me feel kind of like being outside in my underwear. But then my super-Ratman hearing picked up another sound.

"That little squirt," Pinky was muttering. "If he can do it, I can too." And with that he dove into the lake.

I knew what was going to happen. And it did.

Pinky got about a third of the way across the lake—not even as far as Matty had—when he ran into trouble.

He got tired. Then he began gasping and flailing and churning up the water. "Mommy!" he screamed. "Help! I'm drowning!"

Ho, ho, ho, I thought. Big old Pinky, yelling for his mom. I hope Matty heard that.

I let him struggle for another second or two before I went out to save him. By this time, I could hear a crowd gathering. And I made a decision. I was going to save Pinky right out in the open.

That meant *lots* of people would see Pinky, the big bully, getting saved by a giant rat. No one would ever forget it. No one, I hoped, would ever take Pinky seriously again. I started swimming.

When I reached Pinky, I came right up out of the water next to him. Boy, was *he* surprised. He almost drowned right there, just from pure dumb shock. But of course I didn't let him. I put my rat arms around him, under his armpits, and hauled him back toward shore.

"Eeeek!" he screamed. "There's a monster in the lake!"

I could tell that the people onshore thought so too. I could hear everything they were whispering.

"What *is* that thing?"

"What's living at the bottom of Pine Lake?"

"Well, it seems friendly. It's saving Pinky."

"You're right. That's friendlier than most."

I hauled Pinky up onto the shore. He was still gasping. He was scared out of his wits, too. Matty was on his feet now. He looked just as surprised as Pinky. I remember thinking, If Matty has the brains to keep quiet, he'll really have one on Pinky. It will look as if he could swim the lake, but Pinky couldn't.

As I stood there, I heard the voice of little Jessica Kerner. "Look!" she hollered. "It's a ratman!"

I took off like lightning and was home in a minute. Unfortunately, I wasn't able to fly in my window. Too high. I had to climb up the drainpipe for the last few feet. I climbed as fast as I could. All I needed was for my mother to see me like this!

The next day the *South Fork Star* ran its biggest headline since 1982, when Mrs. Bender thought she saw a flying saucer. Here's what it said:

MYSTERIOUS RATMAN SAVES BOY!

CHAPTER 4

And so Ratman became a familiar figure around South Fork. I had never realized there were so many problems around town. People were *always* getting into trouble.

On my second day as Ratman the giant plastic chicken on the roof of Cluckin' Chicken Takeout Ranch came loose. She teetered over the front edge of the building with her huge beak pointed down. Anybody coming out the front door with a 12-Wing Box could be pecked to death if she fell off!

Everyone called her Nellie. The whole town came to watch her totter. Which way would she fall? And when?

I was up in my room when I heard about it on the radio. What the heck, I thought. Maybe I can do something about Nellie. I had always liked her.

It only took me about a minute to throw on my Ratman suit, whiz over there, and pull Nellie back to safety. I couldn't get over how simple it was to haul a ton of giant chicken back from the edge of a roof! However, it was lucky she had reins.

The newspaper had a really good time making up the headline that day: GIANT RAT SAVES GIANT CHICKEN!

A couple of days later, the fire chief got locked in the bathroom. I just happened to be in my Ratman suit at the time. I was standing in my room, listening to people all over town. It was fun. That was how I heard the fire chief. He was swearing a blue streak. I could hear the doorknob rattling. "Blankety-blank

lock," he was growling. "Locked into the blankety-blank bathroom. What if there's a blankety-blank fire?"

At first, I thought maybe I'd leave him there. He really wasn't a nice man. But then I thought, What if there *is* a fire? This was serious. He'd be stuck in the bathroom. Nobody would hear him. So I ran over there to see what was what. The lock was jammed, and I had to force open the door. He never knew who did it. It was better that way.

Then there was the incident at the International Feather Museum. Usually it's a pretty quiet place. People don't go over there much. Your parents take you there once or twice when you're little, and that's about it. How many times can you look at feathers?

The museum was run by a man named Egbert Finch. He looked a lot like a bird himself. He was very tall and thin. He had a long nose and a little brush of hair that stood up on the top of his head. And he flapped his arms when he was upset.

Mr. Finch was upset. I could hear him with my rat hearing, moaning, "My feathers! My precious feathers! Oh! Oh!"

I raced over to the museum. The air was full of feathers. A new cleaning service had been working at the museum. They opened all the windows. Then they opened all the glass cases so the feathers could get some air. Then they turned on the air conditioning. (They weren't too awfully smart.)

That's when the feathers hit the fan.

Mr. Finch was running up and down the sidewalk in front of the museum, squawking. "There goes my yellow-bellied sapsucker feather! Oh, heavens! My blue-footed booby feather is flying away! What, oh what shall I do? Oh!"

Ratman to the rescue! I raced around at lightning speed, snatching feathers out of the air. I even used my rat hearing to track feathers that had drifted away. I could actually hear the sound of a feather fluttering in the breeze down the street! Finally I got them all. Egbert Finch wept with joy. Feathers stuck to his teary cheeks.

By this time, South Fork was taking serious notice of Ratman. People were talking about me all over town. In the newspaper they gave the Ratman question a whole page. "RATMAN," it said. "RODENT FOR GOOD—OR EVIL?"

One day I walked into Weingarten's to buy a comic book. Weingarten's is a combination soda fountain, coffee shop, and candy store. Everybody in town goes there to hang around. Mrs. Stone was sitting in one of the booths with her son Ron. He works at the gas station. They were talking about Ratman.

"Well, I think he's wonderful," said Mrs. Stone. "He saved that little boy from drowning, didn't he?"

"Sure, sure," said Ron. "But what will he do if he gets too much power? He could do anything! I say the police should arrest him."

"Who is he, anyway?" chimed in Mrs. Weingarten. "We don't know if he's a human or an animal, or what! He might even be an alien!"

"Oooh," said a little kid. "An alien! Cool!"

I decided to join in the conversation. I knew it was dangerous, but I had to say something. "All Ratman has done is help people," I said. "He's never hurt anybody. I think we should be proud to have a hero in South Fork. Besides," I added, "we don't know how long he'll be around. He could leave anytime."

"Why don't we try and find out who—or what—Ratman is?" said Mrs. Weingarten.

"How?" asked Ron.

"Well, we could ask him," she suggested.

"Or we could catch him and make him talk!" said a guy in one of those hunting outfits with the green and brown spots. A shudder of fear ran up my spine. What would happen if somebody shot at me? Would a bullet kill me? Would it ruin my rat suit? I didn't want to find out.

CHAPTER 5

So I put the Ratman suit away. I hid it at the very bottom of my closet, where my mother dared not clean. I just couldn't shake the feeling that maybe I was fooling around with something dangerous.

But I kept thinking about it. After all, it wasn't everybody who got the chance to be a real superhero—even a funny-looking one. Super hearing, speed swimming, flying, amazing strength—they were all mine. But they weren't going to be mine forever. It would almost be a crime not to use my powers while

I had them. And time was running out. It was July 18 already.

I decided then that what I needed was a sidekick—somebody to go with me on my adventures. Then I wouldn't feel so dumb and alone. Lots of superheroes had sidekicks. Batman had Robin. Maybe I could have—Mouseperson?

But how was I supposed to *get* a sidekick? Would someone in tights just show up one day while I was out breaking down a bathroom door?

The answer turned out to be no. I put an ad in the paper. "Wanted," it said. "Sidekick for superhero. Must like working with people. Must also feel comfortable with rodents. Pay low—very low. Limited-time offer."

I wrote in the ad that anybody who wanted the job should appear in person at eight-thirty on Thursday night. He or she had to meet me behind the old Burger Barn, which had been closed for years.

At about seven-thirty on Thursday night it was time to put on my suit and get ready to go interview sidekicks. I had taken to locking my door so my mom wouldn't barge in on me. Of course, I knew I'd hear her coming long before she got to my room, and I could probably take the suit off and hide it at superspeed. But why go to all that trouble? It was a lot easier just to lock my door.

This was my first time going out as Ratman at night, though. It was going to be a little tricky. After some thought, I had an idea.

I opened my door. "Mom," I shouted downstairs, "I'm going to go to sleep now. I don't feel too good."

My mother walked over to the bottom of the stairs and looked up at me. "Oh, honey, that's awful," she said. "Do you think you have a fever?"

"No," I said, holding a limp wrist to my forehead. "I just need some rest."

"Okay," she said. "We'll see how you feel in the morning."

Good. That was taken care of. I locked my door and put on the suit. Then it was down

the drainpipe in a flash, and zoom!—Ratman
was off to work.

I was afraid a crowd of hopeful sidekicks
would be waiting behind the Burger Barn.
Wrong. Nobody was there at all.

I was crushed. Didn't *anybody* want to be
my sidekick? I paced around and around a big
puddle, trying to figure out why no one had
come. Maybe it was something in my ad?

Then I saw one lone, small figure coming

toward me out of the gloom. Was I going to have a sidekick after all? The figure came closer. Rats! It was Matty!

I realized there was no way I could talk. Matty would recognize my voice right away. I would have to nod yes and no to him.

"I thought it would be you," he said. Then he laughed. "Not that there are a whole lot of other superheroes around here."

He looked me up and down. "What are you supposed to be?" he asked. "A rat?"

I nodded.

"Do you have x-ray vision?" he asked.

I shook my head no.

"Can you read minds?"

I shook my head no again.

Then he looked at me for a long time. "Did you save my life on Pine Lake?"

I nodded.

"I thought so," he said. "Thank you."

I made a little bow.

"You know, people around town think you're some kind of freak or something," he said. "But I always tell them you're a good guy. I don't think I'm cut out to be a sidekick, though. Since I almost drowned in the lake, I've gotten kind of careful. I don't want to die young. I have a whole life ahead of me as a comic book store manager. Or maybe an accountant." Matty's father was an accountant.

He started to leave. "I just wanted to meet you," he said. "I hope you find a sidekick." He waved good-bye.

I waved back.

When he was a few yards away, he stopped and turned. "I keep having this crazy feeling that you look familiar," he said. "Do I know you?"

I shook my head no.

CHAPTER 6

So there I was. Alone in the world, with no sidekick. Ratman, the lone rodent. It was kind of romantic. It would have been more romantic if my suit didn't smell so bad. I couldn't figure out how to wash it. My mother would see it hanging up to dry. And being a superhero is sweaty work, especially during a heat wave.

The weeks went by, and at last it was August 3, the day before my last day as Ratman. The weather was still really hot. People walked slowly out on the street. Air conditioners and fans hummed everywhere.

My mother had been working on a great big dried-flower wreath for days. Now she was finally done.

"I have to go all the way up to North Fork to deliver this," she said. "It'll take me about two hours to get there and back. Do you want to come?"

"No, thanks," I said. I knew it would be hot in the car.

"Well, then, you can stay here. You know Mrs. Stone is right next door. Just give her a yell if you need anything."

"Okay, Mom." I said. And she drove away.

Now. What to do with the rest of the afternoon?

It was too hot to call up Matty and go someplace on our bikes. It was too hot to lie around in my room. It was too hot to live.

Then I had it. The movies! The movie theater was air conditioned. Plus *The Return of the Cockroach* was playing. It was supposed to be really good. I could spend two hours, at least, having a nice time and keeping cool. I

even had some money saved from my allow-
ance. I could buy Raisinets. It was going to
be a good day.

The movie theater was only two blocks from
my house, so I wouldn't have to walk too far
in the heat. The only thing I needed to do was
see what time it started.

I found the paper in my mother's room
and opened it to the movie page. There it
was. Royal Theater. The movie started at one-
fifteen.

Oh, no! It was one-thirty-five! The Cockroach had probably made a lot of trouble already. Or maybe the nice young scientist and
his girlfriend were going out for dinner, not
suspecting a thing, when—eeeek!

Or maybe the Cockroach *was* the nice young
scientist. . . .

This is terrible, I thought. Why couldn't the
movie have started half an hour later?

Then I had an idea. If I couldn't *see* the
movie, I could *hear* it! I could put on my Ratman ears and listen for a while.

I put the Rat hat on my head. It was just too hot to wear the whole suit. But would my rat hearing work with only the hat?

I adjusted it and stood in the middle of the room, listening. A second later sounds started flooding in. Splashes from the lake. A freight train barreling past town. Birds fighting in a tree. Mrs. Stone humming. I concentrated very hard, trying to tune in the movie.

"But . . . that's not possible," I heard. "Dr. Samsa died thirty years ago. He died in that big explosion down at the chemical factory."

"We all thought he died," replied a man's voice. "But he didn't. Franz has been here all along. Walking among us."

"Not as—?"

"That's right. As the Cockroach."

"Eeeeeeeeek!"

Scary music with violins.

"Look out!" someone yelled. "In the window!"

Crash.

More scary music. Then silence.

In the silence I heard the sound of a match being struck. I could tell it wasn't a match in the movie. It was a real match. But why was a match being lit in the movie theater?

I got my answer right away.

"You want a cigarette?" someone asked.

"Okay, as soon as I change this reel."

The voices must be coming from the projection booth.

"All right, I'll take that cigarette now."

"Wait a second," said the first voice. "I dropped the match."

"Uh-oh. Better get it before—"

"Yikes! That film on the floor! Watch out! It's catching fire!"

"Stamp on it! Stamp on it!"

"I can't! It's getting too big!"

Now they were both coughing.

"The fire alarm! Pull it!"

"I can't!"

Ratman didn't need to hear any more. I threw the suit on, and I was out the window in a flash.

Smokers, I thought angrily.

I flew into the theater before the ticket taker could even blink at me. The movie was still running on the screen. I looked up at the booth. I could see the smoke in there, but nobody in the audience had smelled it yet. They were sitting quietly, watching Franz the Cockroach sneak up on the nice young scientist.

I raced up to the projection booth. The door was stuck shut. I yanked as hard as I could. The door flew open.

The two men in the booth staggered out. Their eyes were streaming with tears, and they were coughing loudly. A big cloud of smoke came out behind them.

People started turning around in their seats to see what the noise was.

I zipped down to the stage and climbed onto it, right in front of the movie screen. The movie was still playing. It felt very strange to have a movie all over my body.

"Just stay calm, everybody!" I shouted. "Please leave the theater as quietly as possible." I was trying to remember how people on television said it. "Everything is under control," I lied. "Please walk to the nearest exit!"

For some reason the crowd just sat there. Did they think I was part of the movie?

"Look!" yelled somebody. "It's the Cockroach!"

A few people started screaming.

"No!" cried someone else. "It's that giant rat! Ratman!"

By this time the theater was starting to fill up with smoke. I had to get everybody out of there.

"There's a fire in the theater!" I shouted. "Please leave!"

Finally somebody turned on the lights, and the audience got the message.

"Fire!" people screamed. "Fire!"

Then the crowd began leaving in earnest. Grownups, children, and teenagers streamed out of the theater. I wondered what to do next. Could I fight the fire all by myself? I didn't think so. I'd have to get help.

Then I remembered it—the awesome and terrible Rat Squeak! The Rat Squeak was my other superpower. It was a noise I had discovered I could make, if I tried hard. It sounded like a very, very large guinea pig in distress. Or maybe like a gigantic smoke alarm.

If there ever was a time to use the Rat Squeak, this was it.

I scrambled up the curtain at the side of the stage. By now almost everyone was out of the theater. Thank goodness. The fire was spreading fast.

I searched the ceiling. At last I found what I was looking for: a trapdoor to the roof.

With a huge leap I flung myself at the trapdoor. I hit it as hard as I could, and it flew open. Then I was up on the roof.

I filled my lungs with air. This was going to have to be the Rat Squeak of my life if they were going to hear it over at the firehouse.

"SQUEEEEEEEEEEEEEK!" I squeaked. "SQUEEEEEEEEEEEEEEEEEEEEK!" The Rat Squeak was so dreadful it even hurt *my* ears. But I just kept squeaking away.

I knew this was the only way to do it. If I'd streaked over to the firehouse, they would have laughed. Somebody in a rat suit, yelling in a kid's voice about a fire? It never would have worked.

I stood on the roof of the burning movie theater, squeaking for all I was worth. Would they hear me? Would they come? I could hear the flames roaring inside the building. The roof was getting hot. I just kept squeaking.

Then I heard them: firemen's voices.

"Let's go!"

"It's at the movie theater!"

"Get the chief out of the bathroom! Move it!"

And then: CLANG CLANG CLANG! They were coming! I'd done it!

The fire trucks screeched to a stop in front of the theater. The firemen started unrolling their hoses and putting up their ladders.

A fireman in a big black rubber suit climbed onto the roof.

"There's nobody inside!" I yelled. "Don't worry! Everybody's safe—" Before I finished, there was a loud rumbling noise, crack, and then a roar. The roof was collapsing. And in that second I knew that my Ratman powers were leaving me. I could feel it.

This isn't possible! I thought as the roof gave way around me. I have one more day! Or— did I?

"Hey, mister!" I called to the fireman as I fell. He grabbed for me, but he couldn't reach me. "Hey, mister!" I repeated. "How many days are there in July?"

"What?" he yelled.

"How many days in July?"

"Thirty-one!" he shouted, reaching for my hand.

The roof caved in, and I fell with it.

CHAPTER 7

Three days later, there was a sad little ceremony in front of the South Fork town hall. The mayor came. So did the editor of the newspaper. Matty was there, and my mother, and even Pinky.

They all stood in a little group. The heat had finally broken, and there was a nice cool breeze blowing.

Everyone was looking at a big red, white, and blue wreath. It sat on a small metal square set in the ground. There was writing on the metal. "RATMAN," it said. "SOUTH FORK'S BRAVE HERO."

I stood at the very edge of the crowd, listening to the speeches. The ribbons on the wreath fluttered in the breeze.

First the mayor talked. "None of us got to know Ratman," he said. "Nobody knew who he was, or why he came to South Fork. But he was a true hero. Maybe he was funny looking. So what? He gave his life for us. Every person in the movie theater was saved from that terrible fire. Except Ratman. And all we have left of him is this—er—belt, or something. And this bit of burned—er—fur. Ratman, if you could hear us now, we'd say, thank you. Thank you from the bottom of our hearts. We hope you've gone to rat heaven."

Everyone clapped. A few people brushed away tears. Matty looked really, really sad.

I felt sad too. Ratman really was dead. He had met his doom in that fiery movie theater. But even without the fire, Ratman would be finished. As I guess you know, I made a mistake with the dates—I was wrong about when I was going to lose my powers. I told you I'm not so great at math.

When I fell, along with the roof of the movie theater, I landed without my Rat powers. I also landed with a big chunk of plaster on my leg. I had to get out from under it or die.

It wasn't easy. My leg hurt. It was incredibly hot and smoky. It was hard to breathe. And I admit it—I was scared. But I pushed and I pulled and I wiggled, and at last I got my leg loose. Then I had to find the door.

It was too smoky to see much. I stayed close to the floor, where there was less smoke, and crawled in what I thought was the right direction.

Then I realized my Ratman suit was burning. So I pulled off the suit and left it behind. That wasn't easy either. But as soon as I got the suit off, I saw the dim glow of the exit sign.

Then—I was out! I stood up. I was in the alley beside the theater. There was a lot of confusion out front. People were running every which way. Firemen wrestled with hoses. Little kids were jumping in the puddles. Nobody even saw me come out.

I walked home, thinking about Ratman's last adventure. At the end, I was somebody who needed Ratman to save him. But Ratman wasn't there to do it. So I saved myself.

A week later, Pam came home from tennis camp. I was happy to see her.

She was just as happy to see me. "I'm so glad to be home!" she kept saying. "I'm so happy to see you!"

"So how was camp?" I asked her.

"It was *sooo* hard!" she moaned. "It felt like everybody there was a better tennis player than I was. I almost never won a game, let alone a match! And," she added, "the food was horrible. Oh, I missed you so much, Tod." She hugged me. I kind of liked it.

We went into the kitchen to get something to eat. I got out a can of tuna and the can opener.

The can opener was hard to turn. I had to squeeze down on it hard.

"I'll do it," said Pam, reaching for the tuna can.

"No, it's okay," I said. "I can do it." I

squeezed harder and opened it.

"So," said Pam, sitting down on a kitchen stool. "How has your summer been so far?"

"Pretty good," I said. I looked out the window. The sun was bright. A fresh wind blew through the trees. "It really was okay."

About the Authors

ELLEN WEISS and MEL FRIEDMAN are a husband-and-wife team whose last book was a novel for middle-grade readers called *The Tiny Parents*. They say they are not absolutely sure how they got the idea for *The Adventures of Ratman*. "I can't pin it down," says Ellen Weiss. "But I do know that the guy who delivers our packages has always looked a little strange to me."

Ellen Weiss and Mel Friedman live in New York City with their daughter, Norah, and their dog, Gracie.

About the Illustrator

DIRK ZIMMER was born in West Germany and began drawing comic strips and making picture books when he was four years old. He attended the Academy of Fine Arts in Hamburg. Then, after traveling all over Europe, he moved to the United States in 1977. Best known for his illustration of funny, spooky books, Dirk Zimmer says he enjoyed working on *The Adventures of Ratman* because he "likes to fly when no one is watching."

He lives in New York State.